SUMI & THE GOAT & THE TOKYO EXPRESS

SUMI & THE GOAT & THE TOKYO EXPRESS

by Yoshiko Uchida

Pictures by Kazue Mizumura

Charles Scribner's Sons/New York

FOR LIBBI

Sumi flung off her shoes at the entrance and burst into the house.

"Mama!" she shouted. "Guess what has come to Mr. Oda's house."

Mr. Oda was their ninety-nine-year-old neighbor and one of Sumi's best friends. She had just stopped to see him on the way home from school and was going to hurry back as soon as she found a proper present for the new arrival.

Mother was in the kitchen washing the rice for supper, and Sumi followed the sounds to find her. There was a nice busy sound and an easy rhythm to the way Mother's hand swung around and around in the pan. She scarcely looked up as Sumi called, and her hand kept right on swishing the rice. Sumi came home so often with all sorts of news that nothing much could startle her.

"What is it, Sumi Chan?" she asked. "Did Mr. Oda get a new fence post for his front gate?"

"No, something much better," Sumi declared.

"A new stone for his garden?"

"No, no! It's alive! It's something alive!"

"Ah," Mother said. And then, because she knew that Sumi couldn't wait to tell, she said, "I cannot guess. You must tell me." And she put the rice aside so it could rest until it was time to be cooked.

"He got a new goat and she will give him fresh milk every day," Sumi explained quickly. "She came on a truck from Kasa Village and her name is Miki."

"*Mah,*" Mother said, looking pleased. "How nice for Mr. Oda."

"I'm going to take her a 'welcome-to-Sugi-Village' present," Sumi said, and she hurried to her room to see what she could find.

What would be a suitable gift for a pet goat? Maybe she would like some caramels, Sumi thought, or a bag of rice crackers. But Sumi wanted to give her something that would last. She looked in all her drawers and finally found an old red hat that Mother had knit for her one winter. It had a hole on the side, but Sumi pinched it together with a safety pin and hoped no one would notice. It would be a fine gift, especially with the cold winds of winter coming soon.

When Sumi returned to Mr. Oda's house, she found him hobbling about his yard, leaning on his old gnarled cane and wearing his big black cape to keep out the chill. His cheeks were puffed with two sour lemon balls, one on each side, and he walked slowly around his new pet, admiring her from all sides. His pet peacock, Saburo, strutted behind him, making strange sounds in his throat and darting quick, suspicious glances at the strange new creature that had come to share his yard.

Behind them all hovered the old housekeeper, fluttering her big white apron and trying to chase Saburo away.

"Shoo!" she shouted at him. "Shoo, shoo!" But Saburo didn't pay the slightest attention to her.

"I brought a present for Miki," Sumi called, waving her red hat in the air. "It's to keep her head warm."

She edged up to the white goat tethered to the plum tree and wrinkled her nose. Miki might be a fine goat, but she certainly didn't smell very nice. Sumi and Miki looked at each other and Sumi reached out to put her hat on Miki's head.

"There," she said, backing away quickly. She wasn't at all sure that she liked Mr. Oda's new pet.

The old man, however, was very pleased with every-one. He clapped his thin hands together and laughed happily.

"That is a marvelous gift," he exclaimed. "Now Miki looks like a goat with some character." And he reached inside his *kimono* sleeve and found two sour lemon balls for Sumi.

The housekeeper looked at Miki wearing her new hat and laughed until the tears rolled down her cheeks. "*Mah, mah,*" she sputtered, "I have seen a good many things in my long life, but I have never seen a goat wearing a hat." And she held her sides and laughed some more. "I'll cut some holes for her ears," she said, "so the hat won't fall off."

"Now come inside, little one," the old man said, reaching a hand toward Sumi. "Miki has a present for you too."

It was a glass of fresh goat's milk, and it was still warm. Sumi liked milk, but she had never tasted goat's milk before. She held her breath and took a big gulp.

"Ugh!" she said before she could stop herself. She couldn't drink another drop, even if it *had* come from a goat with character. It would be something new to tell the class the next day, however, and Sumi could hardly wait to be the first one to speak.

Every morning at ten o'clock, Sumi's second-grade class put away their books and anyone who had some special news would stand up to tell the class about it. Sometimes their teacher, who was also the mayor of Sugi Village, would tell about something he had read in the newspapers. Sometimes he told them about Tokyo or Osaka, but at other times he would tell about such far away places as America or Africa or China.

Mr. Mayor, of course, usually had the most interesting things to tell. But after him, it was Ayako, who sat in front of Sumi. Her father owned the village rice shop, and he knew everything about everyone in the village. One day

Sumi wanted to tell some news that not even Ayako knew about.

Maybe today is that day, Sumi thought, as she went to school the next morning. She raised her hand the moment Mr. Mayor asked if anyone had some news, and she stood up before Ayako had a chance to speak.

"I had a drink of fresh milk yesterday," she said proudly, "straight from a brand new goat who just came to our village. The goat is Mr. Oda's new pet," Sumi went on. "She came from Kasa Village in a truck and I gave her a red hat for a present."

All the children laughed at the thought of a goat wearing a red hat.

"Well," Mr. Mayor began.

But already Ayako's hand was fluttering in the air. She stood up and spoke in a loud, clear voice, and her news was so exciting that everyone immediately forgot all about Mr. Oda's goat. She told that a railroad was going to be built along the edge of their village only one hundred yards away from the school. It would be the first railroad that ever came so close to Sugi Village.

"It's going to come through the mountains and come out right over there," Ayako said. And she pointed toward the windows that looked out over the rice fields. Everyone listened carefully, because if Ayako said so, it must be true.

Sumi sighed and slumped back in her chair. If only Miki had been something more exciting than an old, white goat. If only she had been a kangaroo or a chimpanzee or an elephant. But what was a mere goat compared to a whole railroad? Nothing, Sumi thought dismally, nothing at all.

Sumi had never ridden on a train, nor had most of her classmates. After all, none of them had ever needed or wanted to leave Sugi Village. There was a great clamor in the classroom as everyone began to talk at once.

"Yes, yes. It is quite true," Mr. Mayor said. "A railroad is indeed coming, and the train will be an express straight from Tokyo."

Now even Sumi forgot about Mr. Oda's goat. A Tokyo Express travelling so close to the village was something wonderful to think about. Ayako's news *was* more exciting. There was no doubt about that.

As soon as she got home, Sumi told her mother about the railroad; and at suppertime she told Father and her big brother, Taro.

Father did not sound very excited or happy to hear the news. "So it is coming at last," he said in a quiet voice, for he was thinking of the rice fields that would be plowed under to make way for the railroad.

Sumi thought Mother looked a little sad too. Only Taro, who was ten and thought he knew more about everything than Sumi, seemed excited.

"If we get a railroad, maybe we'll have a station someday," he said. "And if we get a station, maybe the Tokyo Express will stop here!"

"Will it?" Sumi wondered.

No one knew. "I'll ask tomorrow," she said.

As soon as Sumi got to school the next day, she asked Mr. Mayor if the express would ever stop at their village.

Mr. Mayor shook his head. "No, it is a high-speed express and it will stop only at a few large cities," he explained.

"It will never stop here then?" Sumi asked.

"I'm afraid not," Mr. Mayor answered, and even his round, cheerful face looked somber.

"It will never, never stop in Sugi Village," Ayako announced firmly. "My father said so." And, of course, Ayako's father knew everything.

Now the long wait for the express began. Soon the rice was harvested and the fields were prepared for the planting of winter wheat. The maple leaves turned red and gold and then drifted from the trees to the ground. The persimmon grew orange and ripe for eating and there were chestnuts to roast in the warm charcoal embers. The sky grew brilliant and clear, and at day's end the stars seemed frozen in the darkness of winter nights.

Soon a tunnel was bored through the mountain and the tracks were laid across what was once a rice field at the eastern edge of the village. Every day Taro and his friends went to watch the work on the railroad, and sometimes they let Sumi come along. Now instead of the quiet sounds of the wind in the fields, they heard the busy sound of bulldozers and trucks and men hard at work.

Whenever Sumi went to watch the laying of the tracks, she always stopped at Mr. Oda's on the way home to tell him how the work was coming along.

As she entered his yard, Saburo often came to greet her, and she would call out, "Spread your tail, Saburo, spread your tail!" And sometimes he would surprise her by making an enormous multi-colored fan of himself.

To Miki, however, she had nothing to say, for she certainly wasn't going to ask for any more of her milk. "If you could only do something exciting," she would say, but Miki went right on nibbling at the ground and paid no attention to her at all.

"The express will be coming soon," Sumi would say to Mr. Oda, and she usually added, "but it won't stop here."

Mr. Oda always listened very carefully to whatever news Sumi had for him. He stroked his long white beard and nodded solemnly. "It does seem rather unfriendly of it not to stop even once," he said.

Sumi nodded. Mr. Oda was right. It was most unfriendly of it to speed by as though Sugi Village didn't even exist, especially when it was going to pass so close it would rattle the windows of their school house. More and more Sumi began to think of the train as the Unfriendly Express.

Before long, the tracks were laid like a shiny silver band along the rim of the village. And finally, one cold morning of the new year, when the snow on the ground had turned to ice, the first express came through on a trial run. The whole school went out into the yard to watch it go by. It was a beautiful, gleaming blue-and-cream-colored train, and it glided on the rails like a sled on ice, making only a *Whinnnnnng* sound as it raced by.

The children all shouted and waved, but the train sped by without even slowing down. It was hard to tell if anyone was even on board, for no friendly hand waved back to them.

"Imagine," Mr. Mayor said looking pleased, "a little bit of the world beyond will visit us every day."

Each day now they listened for the sound of the express: first the northbound *Whinnnnnng* and then the southbound *Whinnnnnng*.

At first the children craned their necks to look out the window whenever the express went by. But after a few weeks, they forgot to wait or listen anymore, for the Tokyo Express became just another of the daily sounds of the village.

When Sumi woke up one cold morning, the deep furry silence in the air told her that it was snowing. All night the snow had fallen, and the wind had blown it in great drifts that leaned up against houses and trees and made weird white shapes in the fields.

Sumi and Taro put on their warmest winter clothing and their boots and mittens and tramped slowly through the thick snow to school.

It was almost time for Mr. Mayor to ask if anyone had any interesting news to tell when Sumi noticed the strange sound. It was not the usual *Whinnnnng* of the northbound express, but more of a soft *Whuuuuuf* sound. And then there was a long silence. Sumi stretched her neck and looked out the window. There, just one hundred yards from their school, stood the Tokyo Express. It was not moving one single inch. It just stood still. The express had actually stopped at Sugi Village.

Sumi didn't even raise her hand or stand up beside her desk. She simply shouted in her loudest voice, "Mr. Mayor, Mr. Mayor, the express has stopped!"

Everyone, including Mr. Mayor, ran to the window. Sure enough, there was the blue-and-cream-colored express standing very still. And in front of it, standing on the tracks, seemed to be an animal. Was it a cow? Sumi thought she saw a spot of red on its head. Could it be her hat? Could it possibly be Miki way out there?

"Come on, children," Mr. Mayor called. "Let's go!"

No one had to be told what to do. Everyone tumbled out into the hall to put on coats and boots and hats. At the last moment, Mr. Mayor remembered to get his ceremonial top hat which he kept in the cupboard beside the blackboard. He wore it only on special occasions when he wanted to look official and mayor-like. Surely this was such an occasion, he thought. After all, it wasn't every day that the express from Tokyo stopped in Sugi Village. And indeed, it might never stop here again, ever.

Sumi thought it was too bad Mr. Mayor wasn't wearing his striped pants and his frock coat too. But she was glad

he put on his silky black top hat. He looked very elegant, she thought, even though he had big rubber boots on his feet.

They all ran, pell-mell, stumbling through the snow-covered schoolyard and down the snowy paths that cut through the rice fields. The boys reached the train first, but Sumi was the first of the girls, and Mr. Mayor was right behind her.

"*Yah!* Tokyo Express!" the boys shouted.

"You finally stopped!" Sumi shouted. "You finally stopped!"

Then she ran to the front of the train and saw her old red hat. There it was, sitting on Miki's head as she calmly searched for grass along the railroad tracks.

"Miki!" Sumi shouted. "Did you stop the Tokyo Express?"

As usual, Miki paid no attention to her and went right on nibbling at the snow.

Now a door slid open and one of the train's conductors waved to the children.

Mr. Mayor bowed and removed his top hat. "Welcome to Sugi Village," he called out.

The conductor bowed back and smiled. "If it weren't for her red hat, we probably never would have seen that silly goat," he said good-naturedly. "Now that we've stopped for her, we'll wait here for thirty minutes while they clear the tracks up ahead."

The children edged up to the train and touched its icy cold metal sides. They jumped up and down and tried to look inside the windows.

"Some of the children have never been on a train," Mr. Mayor explained.

"I see," the conductor said.

"Of course, none of them have ever been on a Tokyo Express," Mr. Mayor went on, pressing closer to the door.

The conductor sucked in his breath and thought for a moment. He seemed to know exactly what was going on inside Mr. Mayor's head.

"It would be highly irregular," he said slowly, "and I suppose I could be fired for doing it, but well . . . we have only a few passengers on board, and we may never stop here again."

He beckoned to the children. "Come on," he called. "There's time for a quick look if you hurry."

By now all the children of the school had seen the express and they came running out to see it. Taro and his classmates were soon climbing on board too.

Sumi had never seen anything so new and shiny and beautiful. The windows were wide, with soft gray curtains that could be drawn to keep out the sun. The chairs were comfortable and roomy and leaned back so you could sleep in them. There were adjustable foot rests for your feet and little tables that folded up into the arm rests.

The conductor led them through the first class cars and then into the buffet car. Girls in blue uniforms and white aprons were preparing a cart of food to take through the train. Sumi smelled hot coffee and steaming curry that made her mouth water, and she saw real roses in small glass vases.

It was like another world, this warm bit of comfort and luxury that stood in the midst of the frozen fields. Sumi took a deep breath in order to keep part of it inside of her, for a while at least.

The conductor looked at the big gold watch which he took from his pocket. "All right, children," he said. "Time for everyone to get off. We'll be leaving soon and we can't take you with us. Did someone move that goat from the tracks?"

The children hurried off the train and Sumi ran to get Miki. She straightened her red hat, got a firm grip on her tether, and pulled her quickly from the tracks.

"Come on, Miki," she said. "You really did something exciting today, you did!"

Sumi could hear a voice on the train's loudspeaker announcing that the express would be under way in three minutes. Mr. Mayor took out his watch and waited with it in his hand. In exactly three minutes the door slid to, there was a loud blast of the train's horn, and the express began to glide northward.

"Good-bye, Sugi Village!" the conductor called.

"Good-bye, Tokyo Express!" the children shouted.

"Thank you," Mr. Mayor said, waving his top hat.

And then it was gone, and there were only the shiny tracks left to remind them that the express would come through again the next morning.

"It will never stop again," Sumi said sadly.

"But it stopped once," Mr. Mayor said, "and that is something."

Sumi nodded. It was true. And Miki was the one who had done it.

"*Banzai* for Miki!" Taro shouted.

And everyone gathered around and wanted to touch
her shaggy sides—even Ayako. She told Sumi that as soon

as she got home, she was going to tell her father about Miki
so he could tell everyone in the village what she had done.

Somehow her classmates seemed to think that Sumi was remarkable too, because she was a friend of Miki, the goat. They looked at her as though she were very special, and she was excused from class so she could take Miki back to Mr. Oda. It was a great honor, Sumi thought.

She led Miki carefully down the snowy paths safely to Mr. Oda's yard, and then she tied her with two double knots to the plum tree. Now that she was such a famous goat, she must not be allowed to run away again.

Sumi hurried inside. She could hardly wait to tell the old man what had happened.

"Miki stopped the Tokyo Express!" she shouted in her loudest voice.

Mr. Oda, who was dozing peacefully beside his warm brazier, awoke with a start. "What? What?" he asked in a small thin voice, blinking away the sleep in his eyes.

Still shouting because she couldn't stop, Sumi told him how Miki had stopped the Tokyo Express and how they had all been invited on board to see what it was like inside.

"Ah, ah," the old man said, nodding happily. "And what was it like, this Tokyo Express?"

"It was shiny and new . . . and beautiful and clean," Sumi said, closing her eyes so she could remember. "It was as warm as springtime and it smelled as good as New Year's."

Sumi could find no more words, but the old man under-stood. "I see," he said. "I see." And his face crumpled into hundreds of wrinkles as he laughed with pleasure.

He called his housekeeper and asked for his cloak and his hat. "We must go tell Miki what a fine thing she did," he said.

"It is cold out," the housekeeper warned, "and the snow is deep."

But the old man did not care. "What is a little snow on such a day?" he asked, and he put on his fur hat and his black cloak and hobbled out into the yard holding Sumi's hand.

Miki stood calmly beside her plum tree, looking as though she had been standing there all day.

"Well, well, Miki," the old man said, reaching out to touch her head. "You are quite a special goat now. I imagine long after I am gone, Sugi Village will remember you for stopping the Tokyo Express."

Miki went right on nibbling, but Sumi no longer wished that Miki was anything other than her own shaggy self. Nor did she wish that she would do something more exciting than give milk. After all, she had done something today that no one else in all of Sugi Village could do—not even Mr. Mayor. And that was more than you could say about any goat.

Sumi edged up close to Miki's ear. "You are a wonderful goat, Miki," she whispered. "You really are."

Miki stopped nibbling and looked up at Sumi's face. Sumi grinned and patted her gently on the head. She knew at last that Miki had listened, and she was sure that this time she had understood.